FROM THE BIOGENESIS WAR FILES

# AMBUSH
## IN THE
# SARGON
# STRAITS

## LL RICHMAN

# CONTENTS

# About the Biogenesis War Universe

Humanity has reached the stars.

With colonies established throughout the Sol system, explorers hungry for new ventures traveled beyond its borders to colonize nearby Alpha Centauri.

At the same time, a brave pair of ships set their sights a bit farther afield—the binary stars of Procyon and Sirius. Those who settled there called themselves the Geminate Alliance.

Such distances made interaction prohibitive. Even with the Scharnhorst drive's ability to triple the speed of light, travel between the colonies was measured in months, if not years.

In the mid-twenty-fifth century, that all changed. The Geminate Alliance stunned the known worlds with the invention of the Calabi-Yau Gate. The gates folded space, enabling instantaneous travel between star systems. True interstellar commerce became a reality.

Those the Alliance had left behind had formed a loose association, known as the Coalition of Worlds. Though most of its star nations treated the Alliance fairly, there was one in particular that did not.

The Akkadian Empire was an oppressive regime whose actions propelled it into a state of cold war with the rest of the settled worlds. Its Ministry of State Security was rumored to have its hooks in every star nation from Terra to Sirius.

The Geminate Alliance had no idea how thoroughly they had been compromised, but they were about to find out....

Published by Delta V Press
Cover Copyright © 2020 L.L. Richman

ISBN-13: 9798711256960

0  9  8  7  6  5  4  3  2  1

Produced in the United States of America

# ALSO BY LL RICHMAN

You can always find the most up to date listing of book titles on LL Richman's Amazon Author Page.

## The Biogenesis War

– The Chiral Agent, June 2020

– The Chiral Protocol, September 2020

– Chiral Justice, February 2021

## The Biogenesis War Files: The Early Years

– Operation Cobalt, December 2020

– The Chiral Conspiracy, June 2020

## Want updates?

Join my reader's group to hear news of upcoming books, behind-the-scenes glimpses of life with a physicist, and views from the cockpit. And cats, because the feline overlords insist. Sign up at www.biogenesiswar.com/p/newsletter.html

*Citius venit malun quam revertitur.*
Evil arrives faster than it departs.

# ONE

GNS *SCIMITAR*
STRAITS OF SARGON
(ALPHA CENTAURI A)

*{NO SANE PERSON chooses to fly through a minefield. You know that, right?}*

Micah heard the caustic note in Cass's mental voice and smothered a grin. He felt a ripple of amusement from the man seated to his left, but Rafe didn't otherwise respond.

The gunner behind him was only slightly more expressive. Dana snorted, the sound coming through clearly across the network the four of them shared, thanks to the evanescent wire implants embedded in their brains.

*{Not a minefield. It's an asteroid field,}* Micah responded, hands buried deep in *Scimitar*'s holographic console. His eyes strayed to the countdown—ten minutes before they cut the drives.

*{Po-tay-to, po-tah-to,}* Cass retorted. That earned a muffled

laugh from Dana.

He waited a beat and, when no one said anything, shot a quick glance at the man in the pilot's cradle. *{Translation?}* he asked.

A faint smile traced Rafe's face, but his eyes remained fixed, staring sightlessly into the distance, the way all pilots did when merged with their ships. *{You know better than to ask me that, Lieutenant. Half the time, I have no idea what she's saying.}*

Rafe's cradle rocked slightly, assisted by a well-placed boot from the flight engineer's station.

*{I heard that,}* Cass accused.

*{Meant for you to,}* Rafe replied.

Micah turned back to his console to hide his smile. The two were always bickering like that. The captain knew exactly how to get a rise out of Cass, and she always took the bait.

*{You want a translation? Okay, I'll give you one,}* she shot back. *{What else do you call an area of space littered with a gazillion tiny missiles, waiting to puncture your hull? You say asteroid field. I say minefield. Po-tay-to, po-tah-to.}*

Although he didn't know what potatoes had to do with it, Micah had to admit Cass had a point. They'd purposely targeted the densest section of the asteroid belt for their translation to realspace.

It was a maneuver no rational person would attempt, an insertion so exacting only an elite Shadow Recon pilot could pull it off. Fortunately, there were two of them aboard *Scimitar*.

*{This was Command's idea, not mine,}* Micah reminded her, *{so don't blame me.}*

*{Hah. They may have come up with this plan, but it was you two crazy-ass pilots who agreed to it,}* Cass countered, and then tacked on a belated, *{sir,}* as an afterthought.

*{It's the best way to hide us, Chief,}* Rafe's mild voice cut in. *{The brass was right. Those chunks of rock and ice out there are going to mask Scimitar's reentry flare just fine.}*

The clock reached t-minus one minute, and the net fell silent as everyone prepped for translation. Micah deepened his connection with the ship and immediately felt Rafe's sure hand on the controls.

Micah's role this mission was to fly right seat, and that meant he had command of the defense and recon drones. He was also Rafe's backup, in case things went sideways.

Not that the man needed any assistance. The controls under Micah's hands were linked to the pilot's console, and he could feel every nuanced move Rafe made. The man handled the ship like a maestro playing a particularly fine instrument

The countdown clock zeroed out, and Rafe flipped *Scimitar* into the smoothest roll maneuver Micah had ever seen, just as the Helios shed its Casimir bubble and fell out of Scharnhorst space. In seconds, he'd matched the asteroid field's eighteen-kilometer-per-second orbital velocity and dropped them neatly between two massive boulders.

Rafe settled back into his cradle, and switched to the ship-wide combat net.

*{We're here,}* he told the passengers in the back, although Micah suspected they'd figured it out. There was always a slight tremor that passed through a ship when it transitioned.

A two-click was all the acknowledgement they received, but Micah hadn't expected much more. The members of the Special Recon Unit camped out in *Scimitar*'s cargo bay weren't a chatty lot.

Flipping back to the isolated cockpit channel, Rafe nodded to a holodisplay readout that monitored the Casimir bubble's wake turbulence. *{Stand by to deploy surveillance and electronic countermeasures,}* he said.

*{Standing by,}* Micah responded. With a flick of his mind, he brought up the readiness report for the ECM and point-defense drones. Their icons hovered before him, glowing a steady green.

*{The frickin' Sargon Straits,}* Cass muttered once more, but this time, no one laughed.

Micah knew the real reason behind the crew chief's complaints. It was the same reason they'd chosen this tricky maneuver in the first place.

*Scimitar* was in the Alpha Centauri system uninvited.

Rafe sent him a mental nod, and Micah launched a constellation of drones. They jetted outward, flushed from several points along the ship's hull, enveloping *Scimitar* in a protective sphere.

*{Drones away,}* he announced.

If all went well, Micah wouldn't find anything. The Straits of Sargon weren't well-traveled. The asteroid belt strewn between Alpha Centauri's two stars was a broad swath of space—too broad for anyone to police effectively.

*{So, Akkadia named the Straits, but Zosher annexed the area,}* Dana mused as the crew waited for Micah to complete his sweep. *{How'd that happen?}*

Micah heard the mental shrug in Rafe's voice when he replied. *{Don't know, Sergeant, but it's a good thing they did.}*

The Geminate Alliance enjoyed friendly relations with Zosher, the sovereign nation that settled around Alpha Centauri A. That explained why those back in Procyon weren't too worried about the mission.

*{If a Zosher defense platform detects us, I imagine we'll have some explaining to do,}* the gunner mused.

*{Yes, and those back home will find themselves in a politically awkward position,}* Rafe agreed, *{but that'll be the extent of it.}*

Things would not go as smoothly if they were spotted by Akkadia, Micah knew. The Empire that claimed the planet orbiting Rigel Kentaurus was far more likely to shoot first, and ask questions later.

*Better to avoid both situations,* he thought, *if we can help it.*

A notification icon blinked on his overlay. The ship had auto-updated, reconciling its stored maps with the actual locations of the asteroids in their immediate vicinity, courtesy of the drone's scans.

That was simple enough to confirm. He merged fully with *Scimitar*, allowing the ship's SI to completely override his optical implants and replace it with the drones' feed.

Instantly, Micah's view of the cockpit disappeared. There was seemingly nothing between him and the black. His eyes swept the canvas of surrounding space, the SI projecting a transparent layer of constantly-updating telemetry over the feed.

He saw *Scimitar*, as if from a distance. Or rather, his overlay provided an outline of where the ship would be, if it weren't stealthed.

Their ship was a Direct Action Penetrator, one of a handful of DAP Helios spacecraft developed by the Geminate Alliance. The fast attack craft was built for covert missions like this.

*{Damn.}* He stared, toggling his overlay off to get an unimpeded view, of...nothing. *{This never gets old.}*

*{What doesn't?}* Dana asked.

*{Seeing* Scimitar *from out here,}* he replied. *{Or, rather, **not** seeing her.}*

*Scimitar*'s hull was made of a special, tunable material. The nanoparticle surface absorbed all light, making it the blackest spaceframe in existence.

*{Feels kind of like you're falling into a black hole,}* he murmured.

In addition to the ship's hull, the Geminate Navy had upgraded *Scimitar*'s avionics suite with the best sensor-scattering tech around. Its drives returned such a small heat cross-section on scan that it was easily mistaken for a space weather drone.

*{I'll take invisible,}* Dana said, *{but I sure feel better having these on board.}*

Micah toggled his overlay back on in time to catch the RAU-19 railgun mounted on *Scimitar*'s port side waggling back and forth under Dana's hand. The ship's weapons systems were state of the art, with everything from railguns to laser cannons, plus a full complement of precision-guided missiles. Both women had weapons online, ready to fire on Rafe's command.

Micah returned his attention to the drones' feed. Passive sensors swept the area, forming a composite picture of their surroundings, on all EM bands. He studied the reports from each quadrant, and nodded in satisfaction. The scans came back null, confirming they were alone.

*{We're in the clear,}* he reported for the benefit of their passengers in the back, and got another two-click for his efforts.

At Micah's report, Rafe sent the ship gliding forward. As the Helios eased silently from behind the two massive asteroids, Micah pulled back into himself and chanced a glance to his left.

Like him, Rafe was webbed into a cradle, his hands sunk deep into the cockpit's holographic controls. The man navigated the Straits with enviable ease, his body swaying in the manner all pilots did when merged with their ship, attuned as they were to the vessel's every movement.

The ship was ostensibly flown by *Scimitar*'s SI. The onboard Synthetic Intelligence handled the lion's share of the maneuvers, but the pilot held veto power. The merge resulted in faster response times, enhanced by human intuition.

*{ETA?}* a voice cut in. It was Lane, the leader of SRU Team Five.

*{Half an hour,}* Rafe told the woman.

His response was met with a grunt.

Micah's lips twitched in humor. If he gauged his grunts correctly, that one came from Ell, the team's sniper.

*{There's too much dust and grit in our path right now,}* he offered. *{We go any faster, our magnetic sweepers can't keep up. I don't think now's a good time for a puncture.}*

He received another grunt for his effort.

Dana nudged the back of his cradle. *{Nice try, Lieutenant, but the sniper's not interested,}* she said on the flight crew's isolated channel.

*{What? I was just being helpful,}* Micah responded. *{Besides, she scares the crap out of me.}*

He sent the mental image of a shudder, and Rafe laughed aloud.

*{You and me both, kid.}*

Elodie Cyr was a bit of an enigma. On base, the sergeant was about as close-lipped a person as he'd ever seen. She was distant, watchful, and silent.

When she'd first shown up, some of the Marines had tried to

bait her, taunting her about her 'girlie' name. The move had surprised Micah. The woman was special forces. Most people were savvy enough to realize a member of the Unit was off limits.

He shook his head. *We've eradicated just about every disease, and still no one's figured out how to cure stupid.*

Ell did a passing job of it, though. She'd walked past them all as if they didn't exist.

The woman had an intangible, impenetrable shield. Any approach was met with an impassive stare. People seemed to just bounce off her.

With her team, however, she behaved differently. Micah had seen this, had seen the respect they gave her. He knew her reputation, too. The woman was so damned accurate, it was said she didn't need her rifle's SmartLink to take the shot.

And she never, ever missed.

Pulling himself from his musings, Micah returned his attention to the drones.

*{We're getting close enough to get preliminaries on our target,}* he told Rafe, as he sent a small cloud of the small machines floating above the plane. *{Give me five, and I'll have it for you.}*

Now clear of the asteroid field, Micah increased their acceleration until the target was just within the outer limits of the drones' envelopes. An image resolved of a small habitat torus, floating alone in the black.

Khufu was Zosher's most remote colony. Perilously close to the Akkadian Empire, the habitat had tried to position itself as a Switzerland of sorts. It had declared its small populace to be free of the political strife that rose between Akkadia and the rest of the settled worlds.

That had worked for a time, but rumors of impending military action were in the wind. The Geminate Alliance had received reports that a radical Akkadian faction was poised to overthrow the seated government. They'd sent *Scimitar* in to extract their small consulate before things got too dicey.

*{How's it look?}* Rafe asked.

*{See for yourself,}* Micah replied. He tossed the feed onto the shipnet for them all to see. *{Appears quiet. No unusual activity.}*

*{What, no warships? No Akkadian flag painted on the torus's outer rim?}* Cass's snark was back. *{Color me shocked that those bastards are doing things on the down-low.}*

A warning ping sounded as the drones picked up an Akkadian vessel, heading away from the Straits. Micah shunted it to the ship-wide combat net.

*{They're too far away to be a factor,}* he told the team in the back as he highlighted the vessel. *{And technically on their side of the border.}*

*{Thanks.}* A fresh voice came over the net.

Thaddaeus Severance was Lane's second and the team's tactician. The man had come to the Unit by way of the Marines.

*{Any local traffic at Khufu?}* Thad asked, and Micah flipped that feed onto the combat net as well.

He tagged a handful of ships flying the trade route, all of which showed sensor returns that indicated civilian-grade drives.

*{Routine,}* he told the man.

*{Copy,}* Thad responded, and then the connection fell silent.

Minutes later, *Scimitar* came to rest outside the asteroid belt. There was nothing now between them and their objective, except a small space weather station that monitored solar flare activity.

A hundred thousand kilometers away, Khufu was a tiny speck in the distance, barely visible against the black. Based on the data he'd gathered on Zosher's defense platforms, Micah was confident no one would see them coming, but the plan wasn't to fly Team Five all the way to Khufu.

The team had brought a skiff aboard when they'd loaded, back in Procyon. They would use it to transit the final hundred thousand kilometers to Khufu's outer hull.

*{It's your show now,}* Rafe told their passengers. *{We'll be here, waiting. If you need assistance, ping us. We can be there in*

*twenty minutes if you want stealth, five if they see us coming.}*

*{Understood,}* Lane replied calmly.

Where Ell was an enigma, Lane was a black hole. The woman had the uncanny ability to fade from view. She could walk into a room without anyone noticing. Once there, she blended into the background so well, a person forgot she was there. She was the perfect operator.

A cockpit alert told Micah the cargo bay doors had opened. He watched through his drones' eyes as the skiff exited. Jack, the team's only certified pilot, was at her helm. The vessel was little more than a clearsteel bubble, just wide enough for three to sit across. It looked tight and uncomfortable, crammed as it was with special forces soldiers and their gear.

Micah counted five, in addition to Jack. Lane sat between him and Thad, a diminutive woman between Thad's massive frame and the pilot's shorter build. Behind them sat Ell, Asha, and Mike. Asha was the team's medic, while Mike was their demolitions man and Ell's spotter.

The cargo bay sealed behind them as the skiff sped off, arrowing its way toward the habitat.

*Good luck and good hunting,* Micah sent the thought silently after the departing craft.

All those aboard *Scimitar* could do now was wait.

# TWO

KHUFU TORUS
STRAITS OF SARGON,
AKKADIA

ELL BENT TO unweb her gear as Jack brought the skiff alongside one of the many service hatches that dotted Khufu's exterior. She felt the pull of gravity assert itself once more as the ship came into contact with the rotating torus.

The small vessel clung to the outer airlock like an invisible limpet. Thad bent to affix a breaching canister to the seal, bypassing Khufu's security and deceiving the systems into thinking it was securely closed. When the BC turned green, Thad cycled the hatch and the doors slid open with a sigh as the environment inside the ship equalized with the one inside the habitat.

Once inside the airlock, they knelt, working swiftly and silently to assemble their gear. Everyone on the team was well-versed in Khufu culture, and spoke the language like one native-born. They wore traditional Zosher garb over their Drakeskin armor, the cloth's loose, nanoweave providing excellent cover for the weapons they carried.

As their intel officer, Jack's first order of business was to set up their encrypted combat net, piggybacking off Khufu's public network. Once Jack hacked the connection, the team went to work dissecting the publicly available data feeds.

No one would step foot inside the torus without first gathering every scrap of information they could find about its current state.

*{Flipping the covers back and checking for bugs,}* Jack announced, before diving into Khufu's network underlayer. A few minutes later, Ell's feed refreshed and she found herself staring at an indecipherable string of code.

*{Sniffer bots,}* Jack explained. *{They're monitoring the inhabitant's network activity. Backtracing now.}*

A minute later, he highlighted their point of origin. They led straight to the torus's *muhafazah*, its governorship.

*{Someone in their local administration is in on it,}* Lane sent, her mental tone grim.

*{Looks like,}* Ell heard Thad agree.

*{It gets worse,}* Jack added. He brought up another section of code, highlighting the filters someone had installed. They sat dormant on the net, but even Ell could see that all it would take was a single command, and outside access would be cut off.

*{If that don't tell you these* couyon *are about to strike, I don't know what will,}* Thad commented.

*{Coo-yon?}* Mike sent privately, shooting Ell a questioning look.

*{It means 'fools,' I think,}* she translated for him. *{His family's from the Pontchartrain colony.}*

She crossed her legs and settled comfortably against the bulkhead. With a small shrug, she added, *{Bit of an affectation, really, but that's Thad's thing.}*

Her gaze focused inward, on the feed coming across her overlay. After several minutes of quiet searching, Ell saw Jack stir and look over at Lane.

*{Okay, boss. I think it's safe to crack the doors and release the drones.}* Jack said, a question in his eyes.

She nodded. *{Do it,}* she ordered.

Jack touched the door's keypad, depositing a LockPik nano package. The app retrieved a passkey that wouldn't alert the torus's monitoring system that the door had been opened, and applied it.

Jack eased the door open a fraction, launched a small fleet of microdrones, and then sent them cautiously aloft. After a few moments, he confirmed they remained undetected.

*{I'm reading no active scan and no countersurveillance,}* he informed the team. *{Surprisingly, it looks like the only thing we need to worry about are human eyes.}*

Thad grunted. *{That says something right there, ami. Only reason for a habitat this size not to have standard security in place is if someone's done gone and bypassed it.}*

*{Keep the drones sweeping in ever-widening arcs,}* Lane instructed, gaze intent. *{I want to get a look around before we move out.}*

The drones passed through the four sectors that divided the torus—its residential, retail, industrial, and warehouse districts.

It also showed an atmosphere Ell could only describe as tense. She didn't need access to the local newsnet to know things had progressed faster than the Alliance's best intelligence geeks had predicted.

*{All right, I've seen enough. Torus nightfall is when?}* Lane asked, looking to Asha for the answer.

*{Still eight hours away,}* the medic told them. *{We're coming up on first shift lunch hour, now.}*

Lane nodded thoughtfully, eyes on the door. *{Let's spend the next hour scouting,}* she told them. *{Get a feel for things, make sure we're not reading something into the feeds that isn't really there.}*

Her words were slow, measured, as if she were testing them against what her gut was telling her. She swiveled, spearing each one of them in turn with a look. *{And then I want us headed for the consulate,}* she said. *{If I'm reading things correctly, I'm not sure we have another eight hours.}*

Ell straightened. *{The plan was to sneak them aboard a merchant vessel under cover of night. If we can't do that....}*

Lane's expression altered, taking on a grim cast. She looked to Asha. *{You'll be our point of contact with* Scimitar. *Reach out to them. Let them know there is a chance we may need an alternate ride out of here.}*

*{And the skiff?}* Mike asked, jerking a thumb in the direction of the outer hull.

*{Set a charge,}* Lane instructed. *{If we need to leave it behind, we scuttle the thing.}*

He nodded and bent to retrieve the necessary material to make the small ship disappear.

*{Thad, you and Asha see if you can't find a restaurant crowd. Blend in, see what you can overhear.}*

Asha nodded and the big Marine answered with a silent *Ooyah.*

*{Ell, you and Mike wander into the residential area,}* Lane ordered. *{Check out playgrounds and parks. See if kids are playing in the streets.}*

With Mike's head buried in the skiff, Ell answered for them both. *{Will do, captain,}* she sent with a small nod.

Lane nodded in return, her gaze shifting to Jack. The intel spook sat with his eyes half closed, one arm dangling lazily off a bent knee. Ell knew the image was deceiving; with Jack, the more relaxed he appeared, the more alert he truly was.

*{There's a small open market not far from here,}* Lane said. *Jack and I will wander through it, see how the shopkeepers are reacting to the current climate.}*

She rose, and the others followed suit. Lane spared one last look around, before nodding to Jack to open the doors. *{One hour,}* she reminded them, *{and then head to the industrial park.}*

The housing section wasn't far, since the hatch Jack had chosen sat midway between the residential and retail districts.

They didn't see a soul.

"Ghost town," Mike murmured to Ell under his breath as his gaze swept the deserted neighborhood.

A small plush toy lay on the steps leading to a home, abandoned. Down a side street, something colorful had been snagged by a railing. It fluttered lightly, stirred by the torus's air circulation.

The security drones that flew overhead showed the same for the streets ahead.

"Agreed," she replied, voice equally soft. "This can't be normal."

An icon appeared on her overlay, indicating a feed share from one of the team members. Lane narrated over it.

*{Armed patrols in the market,}* she told them.

Ell saw a cluster of three, men and women carrying pulsed combat rifles. They were moving among the stalls, and their mannerisms were aggressive.

*{They're dressed as locals, so be aware,}* Lane warned. *{Thad?}*

In addition to being the team's tactician, the big Marine was also their profiler.

*{This is a recent development,}* he sent thoughtfully, *{but not the first time the merchants have had to deal with them. You can see the outrage, but it's tempered by the knowledge of what will happen to them if they protest.}*

Ell and Mike exchanged an uneasy glance.

*{Hold on. Did you see that?}* Thad asked, bringing Ell's attention back to the feed.

*{Show me a closeup of the guy in the middle,}* he instructed, and the image changed. Thad froze it, highlighting a tattoo, half-hidden on the underside of the man's wrist. It was Akkadian.

*{Enough proof for you, amis?}* the Marine asked, his voice diamond-hard.

No one responded. There was no need. On this, the team was in absolute agreement.

*{Captain, I'm seeing reports posted on the torus's splinternet,}* Jack told Lane, his mental voice was taut with warning. *{Patrols*

*are working their way through the industrial zone, conducting raids on companies that openly oppose Akkadia.}*

There was a pause.

*{Okay, I think we've seen enough,}* Lane told them. *{We're going active. Head for the consulate. Ell, find somewhere you can cover us. Everyone else, with me.}*

A flurry of two-clicks hit the combat net in the wake of her instructions.

Ell drew to a stop, looking for a place they could duck inside to make a quick change. Mike jerked his chin toward a nearby apartment building.

A side door fell victim to one of Mike's LockPiks. Ell loosed a microdrone to jam the building's security feed, and they slipped inside.

They divested themselves of the loose garments, activating their Drakeskin suits. The armor's topmost layer guided incident waves around them, shielding them from view.

They slipped from the building and back out into the street. The drone's feed alerted them to an armed patrol approaching and Mike came to a sudden halt in front of her. She would have plowed into him had the suit's combat HUD not painted a shadowed outline of his position with its predictive systems.

Ell crossed quickly to the other side of the street, Mike at her heels. She heard the wail of a child nearby. The sound was quickly muffled, as if those with her knew danger approached.

The armed thugs rounded the corner, brandishing a variety of weapons—pulse pistols, projectile guns, metal pipes. They broke into the nearest house, dragging those inside forcibly into the street.

The leader of the patrol flung a man to the ground and shot him. A young boy screamed in anger. He rushed forward, only to be stopped by his mother, tears streaming from her eyes.

Ell started forward. *{This is so wrong,}* she growled, gripping her rifle.

A restraining hand landed on her arm. For an instant, she pulled against it, but then abruptly turned and resumed walking.

*{I wouldn't have intervened.}*

*{But you wanted to. Stars, I wanted to.}* Mike's words were bitter. *{It's hell, having to stand by and watch.}*

*{Grav-suckers.}* Ell put as much venom into the epithet as she could manage. Mike's mental grunt told her he agreed.

A park separated the residential area from the industrial complex. Here again, there were signs of hasty abandonment. Balls lay scattered on a nearby court, racquets beside them. A swing creaked as it rocked ever so slightly in the habitat's artificial breeze.

They crossed quickly, moving from the open area into a maze of buildings, uniformly divided by streets that cut through the section at regular intervals.

Khufu's governorship was at the center of the industrial section, the only bright spot of color among buildings of ceramacrete grey. The habitat's flag, and Zosher's, were draped above its entrance.

The consulate was clustered in with the administrative offices that flanked the *muhafazah*.

Ell looked around for a good spot where she could cover the team. There were three tall struts that rose from the torus's support infrastructure to support its clearsteel dome overhead. At the one-hundred meter mark, a skywalk extended, spanning the distance between them.

Ell pointed to the nearest one. *{That'll do.}*

As she reached the base of the strut, Jack's voice came over the net once more. *{It's going down, folks. Akkadia just took over the net and announced Khufu's governor has 'stepped down.'}*

*{That there's code for 'executed,' ami,}* Thad ground out.

*{Not betting against it, man,}* Mike responded.

A map appeared over the combat net, displaying the location of each team member. Ell could see by the winking icons that Lane and Jack had made it to the consulate.

*{We have eyes on,}* Lane told them. *{Consulate guards have erected a barricade.}*

*{Those plascrete barriers aren't much of a defense,}* Asha said.

*{A halfway decent flechette pistol or slug thrower will chew through that in a matter of minutes.}*

*{That's why we're moving to extract now,}* Lane replied.

*{Good, because those goons have now thrown off all pretense and are openly wearing Akkadian uniforms,}* Jack cut in, following his words with images.

Ell counted enough armed men and women to make up a squad or more. Their ranks swelled as the street thugs joined them.

A map of the consulate and its surrounding area popped up on Ell's HUD.

*{Okay, folks. Here's the plan.}* Lane's voice was back, her instructions coming in a staccato, rapid-fire cadence. *{We're going to breach through the consulate's back wall. There's an adjacent alleyway that leads rimward, with a service hatch nearby.}*

The image changed, returning to a display of their locations relative to one another. *{Asha, contact Scimitar,}* Lane continued. *{Tell them we need a hot exfil. Ell, you and Mike are up. I need distractions, and a lot of them. Make them look anywhere but in our direction. Got it?}*

Her words were met by a series of two-click confirmations.

Mike turned to Ell. *{I'll be more effective here on the ground,}* he told her, hefting his kit full of frag grenades.

*{Go,}* Ell said. *{I'll do what I can from up top.}*

She felt Mike's hand come down on her shoulder in a brief squeeze. *{Good hunting and good luck.}*

# THREE

Khufu Torus
Straits of Sargon,
Akkadia

Standing on a platform a hundred meters above street level, a civilian might be lured into thinking the distance provided some form of protection from the conflict brewing below.

They'd be wrong.

Training had taught Ell that this was nothing more than illusion, the kind that could get her killed if she allowed herself to fall for the seductive lie.

The looming threat on Khufu's streets might feel a world away, but if her scope could find a victim, then another's scope could just as easily target her.

Swiftly she knelt and unslung her sniper rifle. As her hands wrapped around the weapon's stock, its SmartLink system sprang to life, requesting a handshake with her combat HUD.

Under normal circumstances, she'd reject the SI-assisted

program, but her job right now was to be a distraction. That called for a run-and-gun style vibe, and that was where the rifle's onboard system had an edge.

Ell accepted the link, and felt it initialize with both her optical implants and the SmartCarbyne lattice woven throughout her nervous system. The process evoked the feeling of something alive skittering down her limbs. She ignored it and rose, casting her eyes downward.

Through her scope, she spied the team gathering behind the consulate. Thanks to her combat HUD, they were shown as 'friendlies,' shadows limned in green.

She widened her focus, checking for nearby threats. Movement caught her eye; she'd found the Akkadians.

This was a smaller group of soldiers than the ones Jack had shown her over the feed, which meant the enemy had split up.

The ones in her crosshairs had dragged three men and two women from a building. Ell could see the terror written plainly on their faces, though one stood glaring, angrily defiant. The Akkadian in charge motioned for his men to separate that one from the rest.

The woman was dragged forward, and then turned so that she faced her compatriots. The Akkadian barked something at the captives, drew his pistol, and then shot her, point-blank, through the head.

Ell's scope captured the looks of shock and horror on their faces as the woman fell in the odd, corkscrew way that happened when motor neurons had been utterly obliterated—one leg folding first, and then the other.

Eyes narrowing in silent rage at the callous slaughter of an innocent, Ell didn't think; she just acted. Her finger wrapped around the trigger and in the next moment, the man who had committed such a brutal act was felled—in precisely the same manner.

*An eye for an eye, you bastard.*

The Akkadians' response was instant. Soldiers spread out, weapons drawn, seeking the source of the attack.

Ell knew her cloud of noise-cancelling nano had suppressed the rifle's discharge, so they'd have very little to go on. It didn't matter. Any soldier with half a brain would identify the skywalk as a possible source of enemy fire.

She rolled to her feet and raced back toward the strut, barely missing a random shot fired by one of the men below.

An explosion went off behind the Akkadians, Mike's work. Just as the soldiers turned in the direction of the new threat, another one detonated, several blocks away.

Ell dropped to one knee and brought her scope to her eye. She picked off two more Akkadian officers, flipped to her feet and moved back out over the street.

*{Heads up,}* Mike advised. *{I just spotted a group of soldiers, headed for the consulate entrance.}*

Ell swung her rifle in that direction just as the Akkadians raked the consulate with a volley of flechettes. The guards returned fire, but Asha had been right about those barriers. As she watched, one of the guards fell.

She couldn't tell if the man was injured or dead, but she knew the rest wouldn't last if she didn't do something to remedy the situation.

*{I'm taking them out,}* she informed the team.

*{You do, and they'll be able to pinpoint your location, cher,}* Thad warned. *{You haul ass the moment you've taken the shots, y'hear?}*

*{Sir, yes, sir,}* she responded.

Ell chose her position carefully, knowing she'd have only one chance to eliminate all four enemy soldiers. Crossing the skywalk on light feet, she picked her spot and stretched out prone, the bridge's cool wire mesh pressing hard against her Drakeskin suit.

With a wince, she overrode the accelerometer linked to the carbyne lattice that protected her heart and lungs during high-*g* maneuvers. It hardened, the sensation uncomfortable but necessary for what she was about to do.

The stabilization of her internal organs allowed Ell to hold her target centered in her reticle without the crosshairs popping up, misaligning with every beat of her heart.

Her surroundings faded, her focus distilled into absolute concentration on the Akkadian at the other end of her scope. She followed the man's progression, led the target, shifted to compensate, and then fired a short burst of laser pulses.

She had no time to check the results from the cloud of invisible fire she unleashed; she was too busy firing on the next Akkadian, and the next, and the next.

Five seconds later, all four were down. She rolled rapidly to her right, coming up into a crouch, and launched herself forward along the skywalk.

It was none too soon. A hail of flechettes shredded the air where she'd recently lain and she raced to put a building between her location and that of the Akkadians on the ground.

As she ran, she heard the deep, muted *kerthunk* of an explosion coming from the back of the consulate, and smiled in grim satisfaction. It sounded like the team's efforts were progressing.

*{Ell, you have company,}* Jack's voice warned suddenly, just as she heard the *ping* of something striking the skywalk nearby, followed by the sharp crack of the weapon's discharge.

Her head snapped around. Thad had been right; they'd identified her location. One of them was now on the skywalk with her. The man might not be able to see her, but he knew she was there, and he began to fire randomly down the metal walkway.

The crack and ping of metal slugs hitting the skywalk's metal frame caused Ell to curse inwardly. The Drakeskin suit could handle a projectile's impact without issue, dispersing the kinetic energy throughout its interlayers and across its full surface area.

But it would sure hurt like a grav-sucking sonofabitch.

As if conjured, Ell felt an impact, the instant before the sound of the weapon's discharge reached her. She stumbled but recovered, trusting her audio chaff to mask the sound of her footfalls.

There was little she could do, though, to mask the *vibration* of those strides. That would assure her adversary that she was still there—and still mobile.

Ell picked up the pace, racing toward the strut closest to the consulate. She skidded to a halt when she saw Akkadians climbing up that one, too.

Ell realized she needed to find another way off the walkway, fast. She scanned nearby buildings for other options. Eyeing the closest one, Ell had her combat HUD calculate the distance.

It was too far to safely jump, but not too far to zipline down. All she had to do was shoot a line, and then slide across before her opponents discovered what she'd done. Hopefully, she'd be far enough along to survive the fall if they severed it from this end.

She reached into the pocket where she kept a grappling hook and sturdy, carbyne-jacketed line. Aiming the unit at the building she'd chosen, Ell fired. With a pneumatic puff, the grapple shot across, its unique hook-and-nano catch embedding itself into the side of the small structure.

Quickly, Ell pulled out a pair of hand grips and connected them to the line. These grabbed the line when locked, but slid freely when open. A direct-link connection to her wire allowed her to switch between the mechanism's open and closed states.

She swung free of the skywalk just as the first soldier pulled level with the walkway. With a mental command, she freed the grips and went sliding down the line, toward the roof.

She was fifteen meters away from the building when the line went suddenly slack. Ell triggered her grips to grab the line and then braced as her body slammed against the side of the structure.

Flechettes began tracing their way down from the top of the zipline and Ell realized abruptly that, although she was invisible, the line was not.

*Well, that answers the question of up or down,* she thought with gallows humor as she released the grips. The street rose up to meet her with dizzying speed, but she'd trained for such a maneuver.

Her HUD automatically calculated her rate of descent, and when the overlay blinked at her, she began to brake, coming to an abrupt stop two meters above the ground.

The flechettes weren't far behind. Ell let go, landing in a roll, just as dozens of pointed steel arrows struck the end of the zipline, causing it to twist and flail in a mad dance.

She lifted an arm to shield her face, as small pieces of ceramacrete exploded from the building's hide in a hail of shrapnel. Sparing a quick look around her, Ell beat a hasty retreat, racing toward the back of the consulate.

{*Consulate's clear. Ship's inbound,*} Lane announced as Ell rounded the corner.

The first thing she saw was a small cluster of people, draped in stealth shrouds. They weren't as efficient as Drakeskin at fooling active scan, but they'd do in a pinch. The team kept a small stockpile on hand for exactly this kind of situation.

Ell watched Asha's Drakeskin-clad outline motion to the small knot of civilians as they crowded close to her. The medic gestured, pointing down the alley and toward the torus's outer hull.

It was clear from her movements that Asha was instructing them on what to do, but Ell heard nothing over the combat net.

{*She's got them on an isolated partition, separate from the team channel,*} Jack explained as Ell drew to a stop beside him. She nodded wordless thanks, her gaze breaking away from those they'd come to rescue as she took in the rest of their situation.

A lone, still form lay on the ground. Upon closer inspection, Ell identified the man as the guard she'd seen out front. She forced her gaze away, continuing her survey.

In the distance, she spied Thad, several meters ahead of Asha. The Marine was moving down the alleyway toward the service hatch where they'd rendezvous with the Helios. He worked point, his weapon trained on the path before them, ready to take out any threat that presented itself.

Lane stood to one side, watchful as ever. She waited for the last shrouded figure to enter the alley and then fell into step behind them, walking sideways, her weapon tracking every door, every window they passed.

The only one still at large was Mike, but his icon was rapidly approaching. Ell pointed her rifle in the other direction, providing Jack with cover as he tended to the lone casualty.

He extracted a cryo body bag canister from a suit pocket, and knelt beside the dead guard. Twisting the canister to activate it, he pressed it against the man's torso and it unfolded, enveloping the corpse. Jack rose, slinging the body bag over his shoulder, and nodded to Ell.

*{You two good to cover our six?}* Jack asked, bringing her attention back to him.

*{Yessir,}* Mike said before Ell had a chance to reply. She turned in time to see him materialize from behind the pile of rubble made by the team's breach into the consulate.

She saw Jack's silhouette nod, and then he turned and followed the team to the hatch. Ell and Mike brought up the rear, their weapons inscribing slow arcs as they walked backward, watching for enemy movement.

The scans of the recon drones showed heat signatures inside nearby buildings, but the random blobs of red and orange remained huddled and still. She felt a passing sadness for these Khufu residents desperately hoping the storm of violence would pass them by, yet she knew there was nothing she could do to assist them.

Thirty meters from the hatch, Ell caught movement.

*{Group of three, coming up a cross street on your side, ten o'clock,}* she told Mike, tagging their location.

He pulled a sticky grenade from his belt and armed it. He waited until the three had just passed beyond an empty stack of pallets before lobbing it at them.

The smart grenade sailed into the street and locked onto the three soldiers. It exploded over them, netting them tightly to the pallets with a web of carbyne nanofilaments impossible to break.

A secondary pop told Ell the Ziptie inside the sticky had unpacked itself, blocking everyone inside the web from net access. They wouldn't be warning anyone of the team's location any time soon.

They reached the service hatch to find the civilians had already been loaded onto the Helios. Jack and Thad stood on either side of the umbilical, ready to spot Ell and Mike as they made their way onto the ship.

Mike was last into the hatch. Ell waited, one hand braced on Khufu's outer seal, as he closed the inner airlock. He stepped forward just as Thad's head jerked up and Micah's voice thundered inside her head.

*{Incoming!}*

# FOUR

GNS *Scimitar*
Khufu Torus
Straits of Sargon

*{We're coming in hot.}* Team Five's medic's voice had been calm when first she'd contacted them, but Micah sensed the underlying tension in her voice.

*{Copy that, Sergeant. We're en route.}* Rafe matched actions with words, sending *Scimitar* slewing into a hard turn. The hundred-thousand kilometer distance could be covered by a hard, thirty-*g* burn in just twenty minutes, but with a Scharnhorst hop, they could technically be there in exactly one-point-one seconds.

No contest.

*{Brace for Scharnhorst entry,}* Rafe's mental voice cut into Micah's thoughts.

The drive spun up and a Casimir bubble appeared. Micah felt the weird ripple that presaged their entry into Scharnhorst space, and in the next instant, *Scimitar* leapt forward, traveling at three times the speed of light.

The ship's SI managed the calculations, feathering both accel and decel so the transition back into realspace didn't rip the ship's spaceframe apart.

Though the trip was significantly more than a single second in duration, to Micah's mind it was close enough that he wouldn't quibble over it.

The drive was perfect for short military skirmishes, gifting ships like *Scimitar* with an agility that gave it a performance edge over larger ships in the fleet.

That agility was clearly demonstrated by their sudden reappearance moments later, some ninety thousand kilometers distant from their starting point.

Their presence triggered the torus's automated space traffic control system. It blared a warning, which Rafe muted with a wave of his hand.

The point defense drones under Micah's command swept outward once more, sensors combing the area and finding nothing but silence.

*{Seems clear,}* he told the crew, but something about the situation felt off to him.

*It's too clean,* he decided. *There should be **some** traffic. Hull maintenance, freight or produce delivery—something.*

Yet there was nothing. The Akkadians seemed to have the torus locked down tighter than a drum.

*{They're not trying to project any kind of normalcy,}* he warned Rafe. *{That means they're either expecting reinforcements, or they already have them in place. They could have arrived sometime prior to our transition into the system, and we missed it.}*

*{Shit,}* Rafe said after a moment's thought. *{You're right. Cass, Dana, weapons hot.}*

Tension wrapped itself around Micah's spine, increasing in intensity as they cautiously approached the service hatch the SRU team had flagged as their extraction point.

He doubled the number of point defense drones, increasing the diameter of the sphere. Merging deeper with the SyntheticVision system, he hovered in space, his head twisting this way and that as he searched for a break in the predictably dull pattern.

An SI composite of a thousand different views encircled Micah. His eyes were their eyes, his hands directed their flight. He pinned drones outside the hull of every one of Khufu's landing bays, but they remained stubbornly sealed.

He sent them dipping through the torus's struts and circling the fusion generators that powered the habitat. Nothing seemed out of place.

With a gesture, more drones expanded out past Khufu's no-wake zone. He flew them past service tugs, tethered in stationary orbit.

Five drones flew out to encircle the lonely weather station, fifty thousand kilometers back, in the direction of the Straits. Micah paused, eyes narrowing in thought as he considered the station.

The SI controlling the five drones interpreted the unconscious action as his wish that they draw closer to it. Micah allowed the command to ride, as he watched the feed.

*Scimitar* had jumped right over it during their Scharnhorst hop, not paying it any mind.

Yet the dimensions of that station meant it was capable of hiding…. Something niggled in the back of his brains, something he should know—

{*Contact!*} he sang out as his scrutiny of the station drew the shark from its hiding place. Two Akkadian Hydras came screaming out, redlining their drives as they leapt toward *Scimitar.*

{*Lane! We have incoming!*} he heard Rafe bark over the combat net.

Given their proximity, the Helios was technically already well within the Akkadian vessels' weapons envelope—except for one minor thing.

The hatch that *Scimitar* was snugged up against was on the opposite side of the torus. The Hydras would have to maneuver above or below the plane of the habitat in order to get a clean shot.

That gave Micah enough time to set a trap he hoped they wouldn't see coming.

He quickly reconfigured the drones under his command, recalling some of the sensor probes in favor of more electronic countermeasures.

Dazzlers and Banshees flooded from the ship's tubes. The former would emit decoy ECM on his command and jam signals between the two fighters, robbing them of their ability to coordinate their attack.

The latter were fighter-bombers. Each Banshee mounted a five-centimeter laser, and was capable of strafing runs. In addition, each carried a pair of missiles, their yields varying by Banshee model type.

Micah called up twenty-four Banshees with upper-range missile yields. He brought them to rest, holding station just abeam the Helios as he went about the crafting of his ruse.

*{That's a heavy hand you're dealing out, there,}* was Rafe's only comment. The pilot's mental tone sounded inquisitive, but not reproachful.

*{It is,}* he agreed.

Rafe grunted. *{I'm curious to see what you have up your sleeve, Lieutenant.}*

Micah smiled. *{If I'm right, it might just scare them off.}*

Selecting a small fleet of Dazzlers, he programmed them to emit a Doppler blueshift that mimicked the footprint of a twenty-five-thousand-ton Alliance light destroyer. He had to gang six of them together to emulate such a strong emission.

A pair of the Dazzlers-cum-destroyers went speeding away from the torus on a reciprocal that would make it impossible for the Hydras to miss once he triggered their pre-programmed sequence.

They exited the torus's shadow with eight minutes to spare.

Rafe laughed softly inside Micah's head. *{Devious bastard, aren't you,}* he commented.

Micah sent him a grin. *{I'm not done yet.}*

Next, Micah turned to the Banshees. He stacked them vertically, one atop the other, synching their weapons controls to operate in concert. The effect mimicked a small salvo of missiles from his imaginary destroyers.

The missile signatures would be a dead giveaway, but he solved that by pairing another set of Dazzlers with the Banshees, tuning their decoy emissions to augment the smaller heft of the actual payload the Banshees had onboard.

*{Nice work,}* Rafe complimented. *{If all goes well, those Hydras will be far too occupied shitting their pants from the sudden appearance of two Geminate Navy fleet ships to be bothered by something as small as us.}*

*{That's my hope,}* Micah replied, pushing his Banshee composite out to rendezvous with their Dazzler counterparts.

*{It's a decent gamble,}* Rafe sent. *{It has moxie. I like it.}*

The ship's net fell silent once more, as they awaited the two Hydras.

As if on cue, the Akkadian ships crested the torus. Micah sent the signal to the Dazzlers and Banshees, and a brilliant blue flare lit up the black, a hundred meters stellar north of the torus.

The Hydras' reactions were gratifying. They pivoted on their y-axis, keeping their sidewalls to *Scimitar* while facing the apparently larger threat head-on.

Micah nudged the ganged Dazzler-and-Banshee configuration closer, and one of the Hydras panicked, setting off a flurry of laser shots streaking toward the mirage.

*Shit,* Micah thought, realizing he'd not allocated enough Dazzler ECM to protect his faux ships. The first volley passed harmlessly by, though the sensor return must have confused the Hydras, as the lasers shot *should* have scored a hit.

He scrambled to send drones to intercept, while sending the stacked Banshees the command to bring their missile salvo online.

A tracking overlay popped up on his SyntheticVision overlay, and Micah fell easily into the rhythm of the red dot and the reticle as he worked to track his targets.

The reticle lined up with the Hydra closest to *Scimitar*, and Micah gave the automated system permission to ping the target.

It was enough. The Hydra peeled off in a sudden vertical climb that told Micah its pilot was likely suffering heart failure at the thought of so much firepower bearing down on him.

The dance was a thing of beauty. Micah sought to reacquire, the Hydra jinked and whirled in a mad attempt to evade the fictional craft.

In retrospect, it might have been *too* convincing, for it evoked a response from the second craft none of those aboard *Scimitar* would have predicted—an action so radical, it froze Micah into an instant of shocked disbelief.

In the end, that microsecond of hesitation would have made no difference, yet it would haunt Micah for years to come.

A tiny flash of blue light presaged the impossible—a mini Casimir bubble, large enough to encase a warhead.

Micah had just enough time to register the reappearance of the bomb at the junction where *Scimitar*'s umbilical met Khufu's service hatch when the Hydra that had flung it exploded.

It was a kamikaze move at best, sheer stupidity at worst. No one could engage a Scharnhorst drive without a fifty-meter cushion of empty space.

No one.

To do otherwise guaranteed the immolation of everything inside that initial fifty-kilometer sphere.

Including the fighter ship that launched the crazy missile in the first place.

# FIVE

GNS *SCIMITAR*
KHUFU TORUS
STRAITS OF SARGON

*{INCOMING!}* MICAH'S WARNING slammed into Ell's head—just as the world around her exploded.

Light, blistering heat, and a shrieking wind surrounded her. She felt the sharp bite of pain, a wrenching, ripping sensation.

There was the confused impression of twisted metal, a flash of deep-black space. An inarticulate sound of stunned surprise abruptly cut off as Mike's limp body flew past.

She lunged for him at the same time her feet were swept out from under her. She reached frantically, desperately, hands scrabbling for purchase.

Strong arms wrapped around her, pulling her from the abyss. Her body knocked hard against a jagged metal edge. Something sharp and heavy pierced her thigh and her hand wrapped around it, only to be prised away by a stronger one.

A jumble of faces stared down at her. She saw Thad's fierce eyes boring into hers. As if from a deep well, she heard his sharp command that she hold on. His mental voice sounded hoarse as he ordered her to *{stay with me, Sergeant!}*

Asha's more modulated tones floated through her mind, speaking in the rapid, clipped cadence Ell had heard her use during a medical crisis.

*Mike*, Ell thought fuzzily. *Stars, it must be Mike.*

Jack's face swam into view, joining Thad's. His expression looked grave, pinched.

Ell tried to lift a hand to reassure them. Asha would save Mike. She was the team's medic. She always came through.

"We're strapping you down, now, Ell." Jack's words weren't making sense. "There's an Akkadian Hydra out there. We have to brace for maneuvers."

Ell's muddled brain registered that last and she struggled to sit up, only to find Thad holding her down.

"Put her out, Asha," Thad ordered. The timbre of his voice cut through the fog, telegraphing to Ell that something was very, very wrong.

"I can't," the medic snapped. "That damn spar severed her—"

"Enough! She can hear you."

*Shouldn't yell at Asha like that,* Ell thought, lifting a hand to wave the big Marine off. Or at least she thought she had, but her limb refused to cooperate.

They both ignored her, Asha rounding on the team's second-in-command with a fierceness Ell had never before seen.

"If I don't stop the bleeding, *she will die.*"

"Do it." Thad's voice was implacable. "That's an order."

Ell felt Asha's hand press against her neck. She heard a hiss, and before she could protest, everything went black.

# SIX

GNS *SCIMITAR*
EN ROUTE
CALABI-YAU GATE

RAFE TOOK EVERY shortcut he knew to get them back to Alliance space as fast as possible. Even then, the trip seemed interminable for those on board *Scimitar*.

A pall had fallen over them, the loss Team Five had taken hitting them all hard.

Micah caught Cass sneaking worried glances over her shoulder at the circle they formed around their fallen comrade.

The Helios was untouchable while in Scharnhorst space, so they'd turned her navigation over to the SI and done what they could to make the consulate staff more comfortable.

The ship itself was capable of handling three times the number of passengers, though the galley and lav remained cramped. Dana had scared up some blankets and passed them out while Cass made coffee. Rafe sat beside the consul, speaking with her in low tones.

Micah slid onto a bench beside Thad, the team guy he knew best. Thad acknowledged his presence with a quick chin lift before turning his attention back to Ell's still, bloodied form.

"She going to be okay?" Micah asked quietly, and Thad's head dropped to his chest. He inhaled, a slow, deep breath, and then he looked back at the unconscious sniper.

"Not going to accept any other outcome, hoss," his voice carried softly in a low rumble.

Micah nodded silently, his gaze wandering to the closed cargo bay doors, behind which a second shrouded form lay.

"You got any idea why their Drakeskin suits failed?" Thad's question brought Micah's eyes snapping back to the Marine.

He let his head fall back against the bulkhead as he hooked a hand around the back of his neck. "Yeah," he said, staring up at the overhead. "I think it happened when that damn warhead dropped its Casimir bubble. It's the only thing that would explain it."

He rolled his head to one side in time to catch the sick expression on Thad's face.

"Could have been worse, I guess. At least her carbyne lattice held...." Thad's voice trailed off, his eyes returning to the unconscious woman on the small, foldout bed. Beside her, Asha sat quietly monitoring, lights from the medical brace sheathing her arm winking in the darkened cabin.

Micah cleared his throat. "We can't transmit while in the bubble, but I wanted you to know that we have a report ready to send, the moment we're in range of a communications buoy. It contains evidence that the ships that attacked us were Akkadian, and not from Zosher."

Thad grunted. "The shit Jack downloaded is a hell of a lot more incriminating, *ami*. Khufu's takeover was hostile, no doubt about it. And we have proof Akkadia's behind it."

"Good." Micah felt a brief flare of satisfaction at that news. He started to rise, and then paused. "What that Hydra did.... No one could have seen that coming. It was sheer suicide to send a warhead in that manner."

Thad's dark gaze met his. "I know. Believe me, I know. And I won't forget."

They stood there a moment, gazes locked, eyes flint hard, in perfect accord. If the opportunity presented itself to exact their pound of flesh against Akkadia, neither man would think twice about volunteering for the mission.

# SEVEN

St. Clair Military Hospital
Humbolt Base, Ceriba
Geminate Alliance (Procyon B)

*Four weeks later....*

ELL IGNORED THE light rap on the door, just like she'd done all the other times Thad had visited. She turned her head and stared at the blank white wall on the far side of her hospital room, making it clear she didn't want to see him.

Being the stubborn-ass special forces soldier that he was, Thad refused to take the hint.

"I see you, Sergeant," his deep voice rumbled as he moved into the room and inserted himself into her field of vision. "And I know you see me."

She refused to respond.

Thad sighed. "Last I heard, in this soldier's navy, when a superior officer speaks to you, you damn well better respond."

Ell blinked. Ruthlessly, she stomped on the urge to do exactly that. Her training ran deep, but right now, her pain ran deeper.

He tried again. "Zosher received the files. They sent in a task force and rousted the Akkadians. Khufu's back governing itself once more. The Alliance consulate service is grateful for what we did, and you've been awarded the medal of valor."

Ell turned her head at that. "I don't want it."

Thad raised a dark brow. "Well, that's good, *cher*, since in order to accept it publicly, we'd have to admit we were somewhere we shouldn't have been."

He crouched down, at eye level with her. "Now that's out of the way, you want to talk about it, Sergeant?"

Ell's eyes narrowed into angry slits. "It? *It?* In case you haven't noticed, *Lieutenant*, I *lost* a fucking leg."

Thad's brows rose, slashes of black against an ebony face. He nodded to the outline of her form under the hospital bed's covers. "And now you have a new one. So what? A sniper uses her brain, her hands, and her eyes to do her job. I happen to know you've got this, that, and the third. I've seen it for my own damn self."

Ell shot up in bed, eyes narrowing. "The cursed thing doesn't *work*, Thad. You know it. I know it. Hell, the whole damn prosthetics department knows it." She leaned forward, eyes narrowed, and hissed, "*And they don't know why.*"

Thad straightened, crossed his arms, and propped one shoulder against the wall she'd been so studiously fixed upon. He stood there, saying nothing.

She knew what he was doing. Ordinarily, she'd have matched his waiting game with one of her own. No one could out-wait a sniper. She'd spent days on end inserted into hostile territory, motionless, observing. Waiting for her target to show, anticipating the order to take the shot.

That was before. At the moment, all she felt was frustration and a helpless rage. She wanted to rail at her circumstances, and Thad seemed willing to place himself in the crosshairs of her scope.

So she let him have it. "While you've been deployed stars know where on whatever missions I'm no longer qualified to hear about since I'm technically on medical leave of absence, I've gone through *three* complete replacements."

Bitterness tinged her voice and her mouth twisted into a sneer as she gestured toward the offending limb.

"In case you don't know what that entails, that means they've gone through the process of 3D printing a new one, and then cutting the Grav. Sucking. Thing. Off. *Three times!*" She emphasized each point with a vicious punch to her thigh.

Thad couldn't know, but her aim was exact. Those punches landed at precisely the point where artificial met original. They produced a streak of blinding pain as each one connected, but Ell's anger overrode even that.

She went to strike her leg once more and found her fist enveloped in long, dark fingers.

"Don't." He spoke softly but the voice had a ring to it, and she knew she was talking to Team Five's second-in-command now, and not just her teammate and friend.

The bed sank under his weight as he released her fist and sat beside her. Warm brown eyes captured hers, and the steely determination in them refused to allow her to look away.

"You think I don't know what you're going through, *ami*? You think I don't hear the doctors talking, see the pain in your eyes?" He squeezed her newly-regenerated leg gently. "I can't feel your loss, but I get it. Right now, it seems insurmountable, but you're wrong, Elodie. You're damn wrong."

She swallowed hard, found the will to break his gaze. "Mike," she began, but he cut her off with a slash of his hand.

"Don't you be giving me any of that shit, *cher*," he warned. "Mike wouldn't have wanted you to quit over this. None of that was your fault."

He braced large hands on his thighs and stood. "Unless you're trying to tell me that you had some secret, advance knowledge that two Akkadian attack craft had attached themselves to the inside of a Khufu weather station and didn't bother to warn your teammates about it?"

Ell snorted, and Thad cracked a smile.

"Didn't think so."

Thad's eyes shifted, seemingly suddenly unable to meet her own.

"Do you blame me for ordering Asha to sedate you before she could stabilize you?" His question came unexpectedly, and Ell startled at his words.

"No, I—"

"She lost you twice on the way back home, did you know that?" He looked up then, and then quickly away, as if afraid of the condemnation he might see in her eyes. "She said it was too late, your leg was hanging on by gristle and there was nothing anyone could have done to save it, but I wonder...."

Ell scowled at him. "There are enough legitimate reasons to be pissed as hell at you, without having to fabricate something," she informed him acerbically.

He chuckled, the kind of laugh that shook his frame. The low rumble was familiar, and Ell felt a sharp pang of loss as she realized she wouldn't be hearing it on a daily basis any longer.

The Marine walked to a chair set in a corner and lifted it effortlessly, setting it back down by her bedside.

"Now, *cher*," he said as he took a seat. "You and me, we're going to have ourselves a little talk."

Ell bunched the covers in her hand—the one on her far side, where Thad couldn't see. She didn't like the sound of this.

"What kind of talk?" she asked cautiously.

"A serious conversation about your future with the Unit."

Ell's stomach churned. Even though she'd done nothing but state emphatically over the past few weeks that she knew she'd never make it back onto the team, she found she wasn't ready for this conversation.

Ell knew this day was coming, and as much as she'd mentally *prepared* herself for it, it was still a shock to hear the words coming from Thad.

"You're right," he said into the silence. "You're a far sight away from requalifying at the moment, but it's not anything you can't overcome. We have a temporary replacement. Colonel Valenti's moved Boone up to Team Five as our sniper until you're back—"

"Boone's a good man," Ell whispered. "He'll fit well with the team."

"You're not hearin' me, Elodie." Thad's voice was sharp, a reprimand. "It's temporary. The position is yours, if you requalify."

"Well, now, there's the rub, isn't it," Ell said bitterly. She waved her arms, the gesture intended to encompass...she didn't know what. The hospital. The Alliance. Modern science in general.

"Despite all our advancements, there are the occasional exceptions to the rule. I'm one of them." She thrust her hand toward her leg. "An aberration, a rarity. An anomaly. They can't figure out why the nerve fibers they grew aren't responding in the standard way."

She stabbed her fingers through her hair and cast her eyes to the ceiling as if the tiles themselves could somehow spell out the answer for her.

"Stars, Thad. It feels like I have acid running down every frickin' fiber. It's constantly on fire—"

"So block the pain out." Thad tapped his temple. "Up here. I know they've implanted that capability."

Ell shook her head. "I do that, I lose response time. In theory, I could block, except when we're on a mission, but I can't guarantee that pain won't impede my performance in other ways."

Thad cocked his head. "You don't know what will happen as your body continues to heal. Things could improve."

"Or not," she countered.

Thad braced his forearms on his thighs and bowed his head, studying his clasped hands. After a moment, he nodded. "Okay, then. I thought you might say that, Sergeant." He looked up, eyes intent. "That being the case, there's someone I want you to meet."

Ell stared warily at him. "I told you, I don't want visitors."

"Too bad." He slapped his thighs and stood, just as a shadow crossed her door. She looked up to see a man, shorter than Thad, with a slighter build. He had dark hair and equally dark, inscrutable eyes.

"Sergeant Cyr," Thad's voice was neutral as he made the formal introduction, "this is Special Agent Gabriel Alvarez, with the NCIC."

His introduction caught her off guard.

*NCIC? The Navy's Criminal Investigation Command?*

Alvarez nodded a silent greeting to Thad as he stepped into the room. He came to a stop at the foot of her bed and gave her a careful nod. "Sergeant, I understand you may be looking for temporary reassignment as you recover from your injuries."

Ell barely managed to keep her jaw from hitting the floor. This was not what she'd expected.

Another physical therapist, perhaps. Or maybe one of those military psychologists, determined to help a soldier reconcile the loss of a teammate. But this?

She shot Thad an incredulous look, and he returned it with one brow lifted.

"I...." Her voice refused to come as her gaze swung back to the NCIC agent.

"I'd like the chance to convince you to give us a try," Alvarez said. "I made the switch myself, after several tours. It's not uncommon for someone to change tracks like that."

"You do know I'm a sniper, right?" Ell's eyes narrowed on him. "I shoot people, I don't investigate them."

Alvarez cracked a smile. "Sure you do. You study them, watch for patterns. You're patient. Your observational skills are off the charts. You're laser focused on your target, to the exclusion of all else."

His fingers ticked off the assets of a sniper in a way Ell had never before considered, and yet were still absolutely true.

"You demand perfection from yourself, and you rely on a spotter to keep you from losing situational awareness. That tells me you know your limits, and when to call for assistance." His hands dropped. "And you always get your man. Or woman."

List complete, Alvarez shoved his hands casually into his pockets and stood, waiting for her response, as if he had no idea he'd just dropped a bomb into her lap.

Or perhaps he did. Perhaps he'd been briefed.

*Well, crap on a comet,* she thought, lifting dazed eyes to meet Thad's brown ones. *How the hell did you know, Thad?*

For the past four weeks, Ell had been consumed with one overriding fear.

It had driven her to isolate herself from everyone. She'd turned away what little family she had, refused to see her teammates.

She'd succeeded, too—except for one stubborn man who towered above her now, a knowing look on his face.

Ell had been convinced her life was over. All she'd ever known had been the Navy. She'd poured her essence into being a sniper, had given the special forces everything she had. It was all that she was, all she knew how to do, all she knew how to *be*.

Her paramount fear was coming face to face with the blank slate of who she was *now*, only to discover she was incapable of being anything *but* a sniper.

"Ell-o-die," Thad drawled, crossing his arms, a slow grin spreading across his face. "More than one way to bag a target, am I right, *cher?* What do you say, think you're up to it?"

"Well, when you put it that way...." Ell turned her head to the enigmatic man at the foot of her bed.

She nodded once, and Alvarez nodded in return.

Thanks for reading!
Want more stories about SRU Team Five? Turn the page for a special preview of the first book in the Biogenesis War Files series, *Operation Cobalt.*

# PREVIEW:
# OPERATION COBALT

**They want a fight? She'll give it to them.**

Katie Hyer was minding her own business, hauling ore for
Cobalt Mining, when a mysterious ship appears suddenly out of
the black. It soon becomes clear that same ship is inbound for
the mining platform she calls home.

When the secessionists on board take Sierra Twelve hostage,
Katie will go to any lengths to free her friends and family—
even if it means waging her own personal war of attrition.

And when Katie goes to war...people die.

— BOOK 1 —

## THE BIOGENESIS WAR FILES

# OPERATION COBALT

## BY L.L. RICHMAN

"Victorious warriors win first and then go to war, while defeated warriors go to war first and then seek to win."
~ Sun Tzu

"The way to win in a battle … is to know the rhythms of the specific opponents, and use rhythms that your opponents do not expect."
~ Miyamoto Musashi, *The Book of Five Rings*

# ONE

CMS *GOBLIN*
COBALT MINING SECTOR TWELVE
BIG BLUE (SIRIUS A)

"FRED, NO! THAT'S not a chew toy!"

Katie Hyer planted her boots against the hatch she'd just sealed, and pushed away from the surface. The action sent her shooting across the cramped space toward the mining tug's cockpit.

The strains of a catchy, old-Earth tune filtered from the ship's audio system as she snagged the pilot's seat with one hand to arrest her forward motion. A reluctant smile tugged at her lips when she heard Carrie Underwood's voice belt out, "*The more boys I meet, the more I lo-o-ove my dog.*"

Jeremy's timing, as usual, was impeccable. The traffic controller who worked Cobalt Mining's first shift liked to spin the tunes during times when there weren't any ships coming or going from the Sierra Twelve platform. Tuesdays were what he called 'country music day'—whatever that meant. Katie had yet to figure out which country the music represented.

"Betcha Underwood's dog never tried eating his own safety net," she muttered as she reached for her pet.

The dog was floating butt-first just above the co-pilot's seat. The netting that usually held him in place was bunched up all around him.

His back feet were hooked into one end, while the other was clamped firmly between his jaws. The remainder of the net waved in the null-*g* environment, yanked this way and that as Fred worried at the material with his teeth.

She reached for a corner when it floated her way, but Fred intuited her intent. With a whine, the basset puppy jerked his head back. The movement sent his hind legs forward just enough for him to make contact with the back of the co-pilot's seat. With a shove of his feet, both dog and meshwork went flying toward the back of the ship.

Katie sighed and followed. The netting Fred was teething on wasn't hers; it belonged to Cobalt Mining. She'd intended to return it to the dock earlier in the week, but the order she'd placed for a baby seat hadn't yet arrived, so she still needed it to keep Fred secure when she was maneuvering the ship—if he didn't eat it first.

Fred thought this was a fun, new game; she could see it in his eyes. His floppy ears haloed around him as he sailed across the small cabin, then flattened against the aft bulkhead when he bumped up against it with a muffled *oof—Or was that a woof,* she wondered—before she caught up to him and tugged at the material clamped between his jaws.

Fred doubled down, emitting a cute baby growl, and Katie did her best to harden her heart against it. Then he proceeded to jerk his head back and forth, which made it nearly impossible for Katie to get a good grip, given that the stuff was slick with drool.

"No!" she scolded. "You can't eat your seat belt. Now, gimme!"

He let out another growl as she tried prying his jaws open, and a great gob of slobber went floating through the cabin.

Katie called out to the ship's Synthetic Intelligence. "*Goblin*, release containment nano, please. Cabin bulkhead, aft."

The pre-diaspora music streaming from the communications console cut out long enough for the SI to acknowledge, and then it resumed. From the corner of her eye, Katie caught a flicker of light as a haze of glittering specks leached from the bulkhead to envelop the floating droplets. A slight breeze grazed her cheek, and she knew the ship was directing the airflow to recall the nano back into the fabric of the bulkhead.

She returned her attention to her recalcitrant pet. "Well, at least you left your diaper alone this time."

She'd purchased a portable, shipboard dogbox—which amounted to little more than a strip of artificial turf with an automated pump that evacuated any liquids deposited—but at six weeks of age, Fred wasn't yet trained to use it.

Intellectually, she knew that *Goblin*'s containment nano could just as easily herd any errant puppy pee into the ActiveFiber coating that layered the ship's bulkheads, but the thought kind of grossed her out.

Katie gave the cargo netting one last sharp tug, her feet planted against the aft bulkhead. It came suddenly free, which sent her rocketing back the way she'd come, her head rapping sharply against the short span of bulkhead that separated the cockpit from the tiny cabin.

With a small groan, she dragged her hand through her shock of maroon curls, fingers poking at the tender spot the medical nano in her body was already in the process of healing.

Schooling her face into stern lines, she shook the liberated material at him in mock-threat.

"Bad boy, Fred! Bad! Your seat belt is *not* a toy!"

Fred looked back at her with large, sad, brown eyes. It was a tactic Katie had discovered in recent weeks was her own personal kryptonite.

She relented, gathering him up in her arms and placing a kiss on his forehead as she murmured gentle, scolding nothings into one floppy ear.

Her thoughts snapped back to her surroundings when the music cut out once more and *Goblin*'s SI abruptly announced, *{Warning! Unknown vessel approaching on an intercept heading.}*

Though startled by the unexpected intrusion, Katie's training automatically kicked in.

"Show me that ship," she ordered as she grabbed Fred and shoved him into the co-pilot's chair, securing him with quick, practiced motions.

The view on *Goblin*'s main holoscreen altered to show the incoming vessel. With a muttered curse, Katie slammed herself into her own seat, fingers flying over the pilot's board, bringing the drives online and sending the tug into a steep dive.

Far from the nimble response she would have liked, the tug turned exactly as expected: like a bloated whale. She saw instantly that *Goblin* lacked the control authority to evade. The only hope she had to avoid collision was to release the load of metal ores she'd just secured to the back of the tug.

She reached for the quick-release, her action sending the entire jackscrew-controlled tow hook assembly floating free.

Now significantly lighter, the tug leapt forward like a thoroughbred released from the starting gate. *Goblin*'s massive fusion drives, now freed from all encumbrances, dodged the approaching vessel with enviable agility.

Katie spun the forward viewscreen to receive the feed from the aft sensors. She mentally braced for the impact between the newcomer and the chunks of asteroid she'd just ejected, but it never came.

The ship, still flying dark, jinked out of the way of the mass of netted rocks, its thrusters firing in a complex series that told Katie whoever was handling that vessel knew what he or she was doing.

The effect on her free-floating cargo was immediate; the velocity imparted to the netted rocks when she'd released them altered abruptly. Katie sighed when she saw that the near-impact had also bestowed a spin to the mass of rubble—one she'd now have to match in order to reacquire her load.

With one last twitch, the ship raced away, its heading now pointed straight at Sierra Twelve.

"Jerks. Ever heard of karma?" Katie addressed the departing spacecraft. "Hope yours ends up biting you in the ass."

# TWO

DAP Helios, GNS *Scimitar*
Decommissioned mining platform
0.9 AU from Sierra Twelve

*Twenty-eight hours earlier....*

It was no accident that the mysterious ship that had nearly plowed into *Goblin* was flying dark. Its frantic pace was due to a surprise encounter with the Alliance Navy, nearly an AU away.

It was a skirmish none aboard the Geminate Navy ship *Scimitar* had seen coming. *Scimitar* was a Helios, a fast-action craft crewed by highly skilled pilots equipped to transport the Navy's special forces teams on covert missions and provide support for their operations.

Today's mission was routine, a training session pitting the Special Reconnaissance Unit against the 76th Coast Guard Regiment. The 76th was stationed at nearby Heliodor, a habitat orbiting the star originally known as Sirius A.

*Scimitar*'s crew had just dropped SRU Team Five onto a mining platform that belonged to the Cobalt Mining Consortium. The mining platform had reached the end of its useful life, and

Cobalt had decommissioned it six months earlier.

It was scheduled for demolition in the coming year, but in the interim, the Navy had gained Cobalt's permission to conduct exercises aboard the abandoned structure.

*Scimitar* was currently holding station, floating silently near the access hatch where Team Five had inserted. Its crew was monitoring nearspace in case the Coast Guard—or 'coasties,' as the Navy called them—decided to get clever and sneak a second wave of soldiers aboard to flank Team Five.

None of *Scimitar*'s crew had any doubts about the outcome of today's exercise, though some were taking bets on how long it would take the Unit men and women to hand the coasties their ass-whooping and then call for an extraction.

Micah listened in on the team's combat channel as they geared up, his duties as copilot now relegated to monitoring nearspace through the eyes of the drone swarm he held under his control.

*{Paintballs? Are you fucking kidding me, hoss?}*

The voice belonged to Lieutenant Thaddeus Severance the Third, Team Five's second-in-command. A hulking Marine with dark skin and an easy smile, the man had the mind of a brilliant tactician and could give intimidation lessons to an apex predator.

Micah hid a smile at Thad's outburst. His tone dripped with disgust, making it evident he thought a paintball gun a wussy thing for a Marine to carry.

*{Dude. These are coasties. Plus, I spiked it with a little something extra. Get it? Spiked?}* Jack Campbell was the team's intel officer. An experienced hacker, he too was a Marine. He was also the only licensed pilot on Team Five.

That came in handy on the rare occasion the special forces team couldn't make it to the prearranged extraction point. At those times, Jack had been known to commandeer whatever local skiff he could get his hands on, while the flight crew aboard *Scimitar* maneuvered the larger Helios as close as they could for the hot exfil.

Now, it seemed Jack had put his hacker skills to use, modifying a child's toy into an offensive weapon.

Micah saw Thad pick up the plastic-handled weapon to examine it more closely. His hands dwarfed the thing. *{You integrated a Spike?}*

*{Yep.}* Jack sounded smug. *{Tag one of 'em with a shot, and they're going to be wearing more than a bright blue spot. You'll be able to track them anywhere they go.}*

*{That's an unfair advantage, Lieutenant.}* Lane Reid's voice sounded as stern and uncompromising as the woman herself. As Team Five's leader, the captain was about as unreadable as a black hole, and half as approachable.

*{Aw, c'mon, Cap, **we're** an unfair advantage,}* Jack protested. *{Besides, it gives us a chance to test out a new piece of gear in a semi real-world application, with none of the risk. How often do we get that?}*

*{You're going to add blue paintballs to our arsenal?}* Elodie Cyr looked as incredulous as she sounded, one hand wrapped around her sniper's rifle, the other holding a blue ball between thumb and finger as if it held a deadly contagion.

*{This is just a prototype,}* Jack assured her. *{And no, the end product won't be embedded in a ball of blue paint.}*

Ell grunted but otherwise refused to respond.

Undaunted, Jack continued handing out his modified paintball guns. They joined the team's standard loadout of carbyne blades, flash-bang grenades, pulse pistols, and flechettes.

By the time they were done, *Scimitar* had arrived. Rafe, the ship's captain, floated the Helios gently up to the platform's maintenance hatch and deployed the umbilical, which would allow the team to egress from the ship into the platform.

Now Micah and the flight crew had nothing but time on their hands as they waited for the drill to conclude.

With the exception of the two teams playing an elaborate game of capture-the-flag, the area should have been abandoned; fifteen minutes into the exercise, a blip caught Micah's eye.

As *Scimitar*'s co-pilot, he controlled the swarm of drones that encased the Helios in a protective sphere. A quick mental command sent the tiny vessels into a tight curve, angling back toward the platform itself.

*{Contact!}* he sang out, sending the feed to Cass, the ship's flight engineer, to verify. *{Two ships, just cresting the top of the platform.}*

*{You sure they're not coasties?}* Rafe asked.

*{Checking,}* replied Cass. Then, a beat later, *{The cutter says they're not.}*

That sharpened Micah's attention. The initial blip quickly morphed into a visual of the approaching vessels as Micah's drones filled in the missing information. He sent it to *Scimitar*'s forward holoscreens.

That drew a grunt of displeasure from the man seated to Micah's right. Rafe's hands danced over his controls, and in the next instant, the slightest tremor shuddered through the ship.

An alert accompanied the action, appearing on Micah's overlay. It informed him Rafe had just jettisoned the umbilical that tethered them to the platform's hatch. A second telltale followed the first, this one indicating the airlock had just cycled shut. *Scimitar* was on the move.

*{Noble One, this is Spartan.}* Rafe's voice cut in over Team Five's combat net. *{We have two unidentified ships, armed and assumed hostile. I say again, armed ships, assumed hostile. Breaking away to engage.}*

Rafe's brief comm was met with silence, but that didn't worry Micah overmuch. If the hostiles' presence extended to the platform, it was possible they'd made contact and were already engaging.

Micah almost felt sorry for their surprise guests. If there was criminal intent, no team was better equipped to take them out than SRU Team Five.

The Helios drifted silently away, Rafe's deft hand at the controls seamlessly reconfiguring the ship's tunable outer layer from a reflectance that matched the platform to one that emulated the blackness of space.

*Scimitar* was now effectively a ghost, with full stray-light suppression on all EM bands. The chances of the two unmarked hostiles finding the Shadow Recon ship were next to none, but that didn't mean its flight crew were going to sit on their hands while a threat lurked nearby.

* * *

Thad had taken a knee and was looking at a pile of rubble through the reticle of his P-SCAR rifle, debating whether he was looking at a trap set by the coasties, when the call from *Scimitar* came through.

*{Noble Two, this is Spartan. Do you copy?}*

Thad did a slow visual sweep of the area. He sent a brief, two-click acknowledgment as he slid back toward the concealment provided by the passageway.

*{Unable to reach Noble One,}* the voice continued. *{We have a situation.}*

Rafe's update was delivered in the preternaturally calm voice all Shadow Recon pilots seemed to have, no matter how tense things got. As he listened, Thad turned the news over in his tactician's mind.

*{Could they be coasties?}*

*{They don't fit the profi—}* Thad heard Micah swear as he abruptly cut off, only to come back in the next instant with an update. *{Negative, Tango One is now closing on the coastie ship.}*

Thad scrubbed the stubble on the side of his face. *Well, ain't that just a fine kettle of fish.*

He turned and motioned the two team members on his six to come forward. When they were within range, he reached out to establish an untraceable, peer-to-peer connection.

*{We have a new player, not connected to the 76th. Assume active hostiles.}*

The woman facing him remained impassive, but the demolitions man crouching beside her lifted a brow, and his gaze slid sideways. *{And here you thought this exercise would be* *boring, Sarge.}*

He elbowed the sniper lightly—or would have, had Ell's hand not whipped out and twisted the man's arm behind his back.

*{Ow, dammit!}*

*{You were saying, sir?}*

Thad buried a smile as he glanced back toward the intersection.

*{We need to make contact with the coasties. Let them know we have company, and the exercise is off.}*

Ell released Mike's arm and then shot Thad a considering look. *{I can climb overhead, drop behind them and deliver the message.}*

Thad nodded. *{Go.}*

She slung her P-SCAR rifle over her shoulder, crossed on light feet to the bulkhead, and then began her silent ascent. Spars ridged the bulkhead's surface in regular intervals, making it easy for the sniper to find purchase. The sticky organogel threads lining the palms of her drakeskin suit would enable her to remain there indefinitely.

Halfway up the wall, Ell engaged her suit's active stealth and faded from sight. Thad's suit kept track of her, its predictive systems using the team's connection to track her telemetry, her position showing as a ghostly outline over his HUD.

That part of his plan in place, Thad glanced over at Mike. *{Rafe couldn't raise the captain. Find her and give her a sitrep.}*

He brought up a schematic of the platform, and dropped a pin on its control center *{We know she was headed here. If she's not responding, chances are that she, Jack, and Asha have already had a run-in with whoever's out there badgering* Scimitar. *Round up any coasties you find along the way.}*

Mike nodded. *{Yessir.}*

Thad squinted at the pile of rubble. *{Stay frosty and don't get yourself caught. In the meantime, I think I'll do a little tracking myself.}*

*{Good hunting, LT.}* The demolitions man rose and crept silently down the passageway, the platform's emergency

lighting lending an eerie cast to his form before he faded from view.

* * *

Rafe had brought *Scimitar* around on the same heading as the ship bearing down on the coast guard cutter, kicking thrusters to maximum in order to gain on the unmarked vessel.

*{ECM, Lieutenant,}* ordered the captain. *{Cass, warn the 76th they're about to have company.}*

Micah was already in motion, having anticipated the order for electronic countermeasures. His right hand pushed outward, his left simultaneously curving inward, even as Rafe spoke.

The movements weren't physical actions; as deeply enmeshed as Micah was with the ship's SyntheticVision system, they were more of a visual manifestation of his thoughts. They also resulted in immediate motion within the swarm of drones under his command.

*{ECM away.}*

The drones he recalled with his left hand docked silently with the ship, while the ones released by his right were flushed from several ports along *Scimitar*'s flank. Clad in the same stealth coating that enveloped the Helios, the drones were nearly impossible to detect.

Micah separated them into two swarms. One went speeding back toward the ship that was skimming across the platform's surface in its hunt for *Scimitar*. The other inserted itself between the cutter and the enemy vessel.

*{Dazzlers en route, Banshees on hold,}* announced Micah.

*{Good. Coordinate with the coastie defense grid to avoid crossfire,}* Rafe instructed.

The Dazzlers Micah had unleashed were tiny yet powerful tools in the ship's arsenal. When activated, they emitted strong electronic jamming that would deny targeting information to the enemy. The drones also blocked communication, making it impossible to coordinate an attack—and, in this case, to contact anyone who might be on the platform.

While the Dazzlers were defensive, the drones Micah held in reserve were not. Where the Dazzlers' purpose was to confuse and confound, the Banshees were built to pack a powerful punch. Their payload of missiles varied by class, and all of them mounted five-centimeter lasers that could deliver pulsed bursts of weapons fire on Micah's mental command.

*{Any guesses as to who our friends out there might be?}* the mental voice of *Scimitar*'s gunner tickled Micah's ear as he watched her target the tangos. The twin large-bore, RAU-19 railguns under Dana's control tracked the vessels the ship's IFF had identified as 'Foe'.

*{My credit's on pirates,}* Cass volunteered. *{It's no secret this platform's being decommissioned. Makes a perfect hideout—or a place to offload goods.}*

Dana scoffed. *{Well, we know one thing for sure. Whoever they are, they don't have the brains God gave a gnat. Who'd be dumb enough to go up against a Shadow Recon ship?}*

*{Let's find out.}* At Rafe's words, a highlight appeared on Micah's overlay. In the next instant, Rafe enlarged the image until the 'SS' icon emblazoned on the ship's ventral fin could be clearly seen.

Micah unleashed a few choice words. *{Aw, that's just great. Don't waste your time trying to persuade them to surrender. Those secessionists would rather die than give in.}*

Rafe grunted his agreement. *{Better warn the team.}*

A beat later, his voice came over the combat net. *{Noble, this is Spartan. Tangos are SS. I say again, tangos are SS. Assume you have company, over.}*

*{Copy, Spartan.}* Thad's voice sounded gruff, as if he were already in the thick of battle. His next words confirmed Micah's suspicions. *{Engaging.}*

The SS in the logo stood for 'Secede Sirius'. They were a separatist group that had been trying unsuccessfully for more than a century to persuade the citizens of the Sirius binary system to secede from the Geminate Alliance.

Highly nationalistic, the group's chief complaint was the imbalance of power between the two star systems of Procyon and Sirius. Their platform promised to rectify that.

The organization regularly attempted to place themselves on ballots. Sometimes it worked; most times, it didn't. They'd been around so long, few took them seriously.

That had recently changed. The SS, as they now called themselves, was under new management—one willing to use violence to make its point.

Rafe sent the Helios breaking north of the stellar plane, giving them a clear shot as the ship entered weapons range.

*{Free to engage,}* he said, *{but try for disabling shots if you can.}*

Micah heard Dana's reply as if from a distance. The merge he shared with the ship rendered the cockpit invisible, transmuting his perception into a different reality altogether. It was as if he floated freely in the black, his view unimpeded by something as mundane as bulkhead and hull.

Over comms, he heard Cass coordinating with the coastie defense grid, updating them in real-time of *Scimitar*'s intentions.

*Scimitar* surged forward. The next few minutes passed by in a blur, yet held that quality of time slowing that so often happened when senses were acute.

Although *Scimitar* was invisible to EM scans, Dana's railgun fire easily marked the Helios' location. The SS vessel returned fire, and Rafe slewed to port, tracer rounds from the enemy ship flashing by.

Micah swiveled his head to follow the other spacecraft as it began evasive maneuvers, the reticle of his Banshee's targeting app locking onto the enemy ship with smooth precision. With a thought, the drone under his command spat out a series of two-second bursts, pulsed light from its five-centimeter laser hitting the seam where the fusion drive met its powerplant.

The Banshee's initial assault weakened the area just enough that the follow-up missile Micah unleashed punched through the outer hull, severing its drive train. The other craft disintegrated instantly.

Even as the debris field expanded, Rafe was already banking *Scimitar* into a tight curve.

*{What part of* **disabling** *shots did you not understand, Lieutenant?}*

*{That ship shouldn't have blown like it did.}* Micah spared a swift glance at the man seated to his right. *{It's almost as if they had some sort of dead-man's switch wired in to ensure no prisoners were taken.}*

*{Survivors?}* Rafe barked the question at Cass as the ship carved an arc that took them below the plane of the system, neatly avoiding the debris field.

Out of the corner of his eye, Micah saw the crew chief shake her head. *{It must have been remotely piloted, I'm not reading any biological material in the field at all.}*

*{Huh. Anyone else think this was a bit too easy?}* Dana spoke into the silence.

A quick blip caught Micah's eye. At the same time, Cass let out a string of curses. *{Dana, next time, keep your damn mouth shut.}*

Three more ships swept out from behind a well-positioned asteroid whose metal content had effectively blocked their ship's scan from reading them.

*{Brace for maneuvers!}*

Find out what happens to Katie, Fred, and the recon team aboard *Wraith* in *Operation Cobalt*, available now on Amazon and in Kindle Unlimited.

For more information on upcoming releases or the latest news on space science and technology, like LL Richman's Facebook page, join the Biogenesis War Friends and Fans group, or join the Biogenesis War reader's group at https://www.biogenesiswar.com/p/newsletter.html

# TERMINOLOGY

**DUET Wires (aka "the wire")** – DUET stands for Direct Uplink Evanescent Telecom. Much to the dismay of the corporation that invented the tech, that name never took hold. Commonly known simply as 'the wire,' a DUET implant is embedded within every human when they come of age, and is included as a part of the educational system of most sovereign star nations.

Receiving a wire must wait until the brain has reached certain development criteria, as its integration evolves after the initial implant.

**Calabi-Yau Gate** – This method of folding space bends the compactified branes stacked within the Bulk of hyperspace, allowing for instantaneous travel in normal spacetime, from one location to another, regardless of distance.

**Scharnhorst Drive** – The Scharnhorst is an interstellar drive that generates a Casimir bubble. This allows the drive to harness the Scharnhorst effect,  a phenomenon in which light travels faster than c. The drive allows a ship inside its bubble to travel at triple the speed of light.

**SmartCarbyne Nanofloss** – Carbyne, a chain of single carbon atoms, has twice the tensile strength of graphene. A lattice of ultrafine carbyne filaments, when implanted, will reinforce bone, muscle, and sinew.
Some branches of the Geminate Navy receive a variant of carbyne nanofloss, which functions as an endoskeleton implant.

SmartCarbyne is a unique variant, capable of altering its state. It was originally created to protect military pilots during high-g maneuvers. Its ability to turn 'on' and 'off' made it ideal for protecting the soft tissues of vital organs.

A SmartCarbyne lattice is controlled by an implanted accelerometer. When disengaged, the atoms are in a disorganized, soft state. When experiencing acceleration greater than what the human body can withstand, the lattice automatically hardens, protecting the pilot.

**Ziptie** – The Ziptie is a nano breach application used as a restraint. Once placed onto exposed flesh, the app immediately unpacks itself, blocking an individual's wire from transmitting a call for help, and rendering body augmentation inert. A military version can take control of a soldier's SmartCarbyne endoskeleton, rendering the victim temporarily immobile.

# WEAPONRY & ARMOR

**CUSP** – Compact Ultra-Short Pulse pistol uses a pulsed, laser-induced plasma to either paralyze, flash-bang, flash-blind, or deliver searing pain, depending on the weapon's setting.

**P-SCAR** – Pulsed Special Combat Assault Rifle.

**RAU-19** – Railgun mounted on DAP Helios attack craft.

# ALSO BY LL RICHMAN

You can always find the most up to date listing of book titles on LL Richman's Amazon Author Page.

## The Biogenesis War

– The Chiral Agent, June 2020

– The Chiral Protocol, September 2020

– Chiral Justice, February 2021

## The Biogenesis War Files: The Early Years

– Operation Cobalt, December 2020

– The Chiral Conspiracy, June 2020

## Want updates?

Join my reader's group to hear news of upcoming books, behind-the-scenes glimpses of life with a physicist, and views from the cockpit. And cats, because the feline overlords insist. Sign up at bit.ly/biogenesiswar.

# ABOUT THE AUTHOR

L.L. Richman has a diverse career background, having spent more than a decade working in radiation physics, and twice that as a director of film and video. An avid pilot and photographer, Richman can often be found flying a Piper Cherokee or photographing Deep Sky Objects (DSOs) late at night.

For more information on upcoming releases or the latest news on space science and technology, like LL Richman's Facebook page, join the Biogenesis War Friends and Fans group, or subscribe to the mailing list.

www.ingramcontent.com/pod-product-compliance
Lightning Source LLC
Chambersburg PA
CBHW021340160726
47994CB00007B/2788